little Bird's
A B C

For Catherientjie

Copyright © Piet Grobler 2005
Originally published by Lemniscaat b.v. Rotterdam
Under the title *Het vogeltjes ABC*
All rights reserved
Printed in Belgium
CIP data available
First U.S. edition

little Bird's

piet grobler

Front Street & Lemniscaat

Burp...

Chirp chirp chirp

Doink!

Jeepers creepers!

Mmmm.....

Plop.

Rtrrrrr.....

Tok-tok-tok

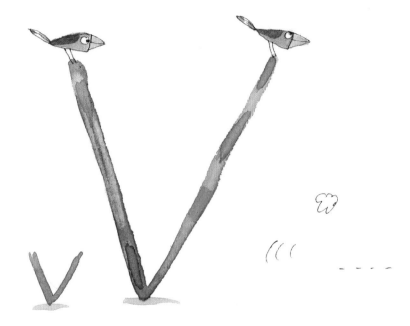

Vroom, vroom!

Yaaawwwn

Zzzz....